KU-165-732

THE RAILWAY SERIES NO. 34

Jock the New Engine

CHRISTOPHER AWDRY

with illustrations by

CLIVE SPONG

HEINEMANN · LONDON

The author and publisher are grateful to Mr Douglas Ferreira
and fellow members of The Ravenglass & Eskdale Railway,
Cumbria, for help in the preparation of this book.

William Heinemann Ltd
Michelin House
81 Fulham Road
London SW3 6RB

LONDON   MELBOURNE   AUCKLAND

First published in 1990
Copyright © William Heinemann Ltd 1990
Reprinted 1991
ISBN 0 434 97611 3

Printed and bound in Great Britain by
William Clowes Limited, Beccles and London

Dear Friends,

The Arlesdale Railway is a narrow-gauge line which runs inland along a beautiful valley. It starts at the terminus of Duck's branch line, and Duck and Oliver bring many visitors. So many, in fact, that Rex, Bert and Mike found that they couldn't carry them all on their own. And that is why Jock was built. I like Jock – I hope you will too.

THE AUTHOR

We Need Another Engine

Rex, Bert and Mike, the Small Railway Engines, were excited. The Thin Clergyman had written a book about them, and today it was going to be published.

"Am I in it?" asked Frank. He was a diesel, and inclined to be grumpy.

The Small Controller shook his head.

"I'm sorry," he said. "You weren't here when the Thin Clergyman wrote it, I'm afraid, so he didn't know about you."

Frank was cross. When his driver came to start him the next day, he refused to go.

"It's not fair," Frank grumbled. "Why can't I be in a book like the others?"

"Cheer up," said his driver. "It's only a book!"

"It's got pictures, hasn't it," muttered Frank. "I'm not in them either, I suppose."

"Come on, Frank," said his driver, losing patience. "It's teamwork that counts on a railway, not books." He pressed the starter button again.

"Don't care," growled Frank, and started suddenly. He jerked forward. Before his driver could stop him, Frank hit the wall at the back of the shed.

Frank was unhurt, but one of the shed supports was cracked. He was sorry at once, and even sorrier when he realised that the Small Controller had just come into the shed. The Small Controller was cross, and ordered Frank out to work while he made sure that the shed was safe.

That afternoon Rex left the bottom station with a heavy train. As they climbed the first hill his driver watched the steam gauge anxiously.

"We've got a steam leak somewhere," he said.

They stopped in a loop to let Mike pass. That helped, but Rex was exhausted when they reached the Green. He hardly noticed Frank, working in the siding.

"I think we can make it to the top," encouraged his driver.

But they didn't. They had to stop in the next loop, and the driver switched on his radio-telephone. Engines on the Small Railway are now fitted with radio-telephones. Their drivers can talk to Control, who can then make sure that the trains run safely.

"Rex has got a badly-leaking steampipe," reported the driver to Control. "We're all right on our own, but the train is too much for us. Can you help, please?"

"We'll get you out somehow," said Control. "Don't go away."

"Very funny," muttered Rex. "Chance would be a fine thing."

Bert passed, with a down train.

"Overworked, that's what we are," he sympathised. "We need another engine."

About ten minutes later Rex heard a cheerful toot from behind, and Frank rumbled through the loop.

"Wonderful things, these radios," said Frank. "Control says you need help – I'm to take the train and let you go home alone. Teamwork, my driver calls it."

Frank ran ahead and Rex was uncoupled and backed into the loop. Frank reversed on to the train, and, when everything was ready, set off for the top station.

Rex hurried home, and his driver set to work to mend the broken steampipe. The job took a long time.

"If only we had a spare engine," grumbled the driver.

At the top station Frank's driver apologised to the passengers for being late, but they didn't mind.

"You put things right very well," they said. "We were expecting a walk home."

The Small Controller was pleased too.

"Well done Frank," he said. "And the shed is not badly damaged either, so we'll say no more about it."

But he was thoughtful as he went back to his office.

"Frank shouldn't have to do rescue acts," he said to himself. "We *do* need another engine."

Sticking-Power

The holiday season was drawing to a close. It had been a busy year, and Bert was feeling unwell.

Rex and Mike were unsympathetic.

"Poor old Bert," they said to each other. "A shame he's out of puff. No stamina, these youngsters. What you need, Bert," Mike went on, "is determination and sticking-power."

"Sticking-power be blowed. I might have known I'd get no sympathy from you two," grumbled Bert.

"I can't get my breath properly," Bert complained to his fitter.

"You need new tubes," the fitter said, "but we can't spare you at present. Keep going, and we'll give you a new set during the winter." He paused and looked over his shoulder. "Keep it under your dome," he said quietly, "but I did hear rumours about a new engine. We need one, because if any of you three failed we'd really be in trouble."

He gave Bert's tubes a good clean. This helped a little, but Bert soon felt poorly again.

Bert did his best, and one afternoon he reached the top station feeling very pleased with himself. His train was full, yet he had lost only a few minutes on the journey.

His driver put him onto the turntable and he ran eagerly round his coaches.

"That gives me time for a good breather before we go down again," he said to himself.

He simmered happily as he waited for the guard to blow his whistle and wave his green flag.

There was a hill near the station, and Bert knew that once he was over it he could run home without losing time.

The green flag waved at last.

"Come on," puffed Bert. "Come on, come on, come . . . oh!" Suddenly there was a jerk and everything seemed easy. Bert's driver looked back.

"Whoa," he groaned. "Back we go! We've left our train behind."

The Guard met them.

"The tender coupling's broken," he said. "We'll just have to stick around until someone can bring up a spare."

"Stick around!" grumbled Bert crossly. "I know what Rex and Mike will say about sticking!"

His driver looked at him.

"Hey!" he exclaimed. "You've given me an idea."

He disappeared into the station shop, and returned carrying a small box.

"Glue," he explained. "It's supposed to stick anything."

"Even trains?" snorted Bert disbelievingly. His driver ignored him and set to work.

"Now I've heard everything," muttered Bert. Then an idea came to him, and he smiled.

"That'll stop their teasing," he said to himself.

At last the job was done.

"There's no hurry," said Bert's driver. "We'll take it steadily and make sure the passengers get home. The guard has told them what has happened, and they say they don't mind being late."

The hill near the station was the difficult part. Gently, carefully, Bert eased the train over it. After that, though he took care, it was with growing confidence that he trundled the train home. The passengers all congratulated him and gave him three cheers.

When Rex and Mike came into the Shed that evening they looked tired.

"Phew!" remarked Mike. "Thank goodness we're not as busy as that every day."

Bert grinned.

"Sorry you're tired," he said brightly. "I thought you older engines had sticking-power. What you need is . . . " and he told them about his adventure with the glue.

"So that's sticking-power," he finished. "Never mind – some of us have it and some of us don't. Goodnight." And he went happily to sleep.

Jock

"Do you know what I think?" asked Bert one evening, soon after the next season began.

"News to me that you could," said Mike cheekily.

"I suppose it would be," retorted Bert, "never having done any thinking yourself."

Rex chuckled, and he and Mike waited.

"Well, go on," prompted Mike at last. "Aren't you going to impress us with your thoughts after all?" He winked at Rex.

"Something," Bert announced after another pause, "is going on in the workshop."

"Work?" suggested Rex innocently. Bert took no notice.

"I think," went on Bert, "that the men are building something. I was waiting at the platform yesterday and the workshop door was open. I couldn't see much, but there was something on the floor inside – it looked liked a boiler."

"Is that all?" said Rex. He sounded disappointed.

"Probably a spare for one of us," said Mike.

"I don't think so," argued Bert. "There were wheels as well. What I think . . . " – he paused dramatically – " . . . is that they're building a new engine."

"My fitter said he'd heard a rumour," added Bert.

Three Small Engines looked hopefully at each other.

"About time too," said Rex.

"What's the new engine's name?" Mike asked his driver the next morning.

"How did you know about the new engine?" the driver asked. "It's supposed to be a secret."

They told him, and he laughed.

"I don't think the Small Controller has chosen a name yet," he said. "When he does I'll let you know."

But a few weeks later, when the new engine came out of the workshop for tests, the Small Controller had still not decided on a name.

"How odd," remarked Mike, looking with interest at the new engine's square windows and square-topped dome.

"And what a funny colour," put in Rex.

"No, it's not," said Bert. "I like it."

The new engine smiled.

"So do I," he said. "My driver says it will be different in the end – this is something he calls an undercoat."

Douglas and Duck came to look too. Douglas had just brought some empty ballast trucks along the branch line: he and Duck watched with interest as the new engine was put through his paces.

"He puts me in mind of ma days in Scotland," Douglas remarked. "Some o' the engines up in the Highlands were yon colour. Jocks, we used to call them."

"Jocks?" asked the new engine, stopping nearby.

"Aye," agreed Douglas. "No' a bad name for yoursel' I'm thinking, eh, Jock?"

The Small Controller was delighted.

"Well done, Douglas," he said, and turned to the new engine. "What do you think?" he asked. "It means you'd have to keep your colour too, to give the name some point. Would you mind?"

"Not a bit, Sir," said the new engine. "I like the colour, and the name would suit me fine."

"Excellent," said the Small Controller. That's settled then. Thank you, Douglas – a splendid idea."

And Douglas puffed away, well satisfied with his morning's work.

Teamwork

All the tests on Jock went without a hitch, and when the holiday months came, the new engine had already proved his value. He was stronger than the others, and people even came to the railway on purpose to see him. Unfortunately this went to his smokebox, and he became rather cocky.

One day Jock was alone at the bottom station. A container of sleepers arrived, but the lorry could not get into the yard.

"Now what?" demanded the lorry driver, scratching his head.

"No problem," said the Small Controller. "Just arrange the trailer astride the rails, and leave it. Jock will do the rest."

A cable was fastened between Jock's tender and the trailer, and, puffing hard, Jock pulled the trailer into the Yard.

"Road or rail, what do I care," Jock boasted in the shed that night. The engines looked at each other in dismay.

Next day Mike was waiting at the platform to take a train up the line, when he saw Jock backing down towards him.

"What's this?" he asked as Jock was coupled on. "I can manage."

"The Small Controller wants me to help," said Jock importantly. "The party on the train has asked to see me specially."

"Oh has it?" said Mike. "Well make sure you don't leave me to push you as well as pull the train."

That gave Mike an idea. He whispered to his driver, who grinned and nodded.

"We'll do it after the Green," he said.

So when they re-started from the Green, he gradually cut off steam . . .

Now the whole weight of the train, with Mike as well, pulled on Jock's coupling. Smoke and steam shot high in the air as he had to work extra hard. Jock's driver glanced back. When he saw Mike grinning he realised what was happening.

"Feeling tired are you, Mike?" asked Jock at the top station.

"You were enjoying yourself," Mike grinned. "I didn't want to spoil your fun."

"Ah," said Jock. "I wondered if perhaps I was going too fast for you . . ."

"Too fast!" spluttered Mike. "You wait!"

But Jock didn't wait – he chuckled, and ran quickly away so that Mike could have his turn on the 'table'.

Mike was still cross when it was time to leave, and started at a great pace.

"Steady," said his driver. "We're not racing anyone."

"That's what you think," muttered Mike.

They stopped at the Green. Mike's driver tried to let water into the boiler, but the injector wouldn't work.

"Ouch," squeaked Mike. "Give me a drink quickly, please – I think I'm going to burst."

"Your injector has failed," explained the driver, turning to his radio-telephone. "Now Jock will have to pull us home."

"What!" spluttered Mike, but there was no other way. Mike's fire was put out, Jock moved to the front of the train, and in the end little time was lost. Duck, warned by Control, was waiting for any passengers who wanted to go to the Big Station.

Mike went to the shed to be mended, and was feeling better by the time the others arrived.

"I'm sorry I made you do all the work this morning," Mike apologised when Jock came in. "Thank you for bringing me home."

"That's all right," said Jock. "I'm sorry too. It's silly trying to get the better of each other – if I hadn't teased you perhaps your injector wouldn't have failed. It taught me a lesson. On a railway it's teamwork that counts."

The other three small engines agreed, and, looking at them, Jock was glad that he was one of the team.